our last cigarette

By Mingeli

ISBN: 978-1-7764833-2-7 (Paperback)
ISBN: 978-1-7764834-2-6 (Ebook)

This book is a work of fiction, and therefore all characters, names, and locations are fictional and imaginary. Any resemblance to any true event, person, etc. is purely coincidental and not intentional. Additionally, this work is not intended to offend or defame any nationalities, community, religion, culture/tradition, political or any person(s) living or dead.

Trigger Warning: This book explores themes around mental health topics such as depression, anxiety, self-harm, suicide, and death.

For permission requests and collaboration:

dearmingeli@gmail.com

This is our last cigarette, so if it's okay, may we never meet again.

By Mingeli,

Poetry.

1. Are You Jealous That I Am Sad Without You?

2. But Who Loves Sad Boys?

3. Find Me In The Land Of Venus And Milk.

4. Infinite Hurrahs To Us Broken Things.

5. We Are Not Allowed To Die Here.

6. The Melancholy District Is Falling.

7. Someone Has To Love Your Ghost.

8. Sad Boy Politics.

9. Ukiyo: And we run 'til we die.

10. We Were Never Ugly To Begin With.

The author celebrates 10 published titles and over 1000 poems. This collection is a compilation of the readers' and Mingeli's 10 favourite poems from each book, with some reconstructed in a way to fit the title 'Our Last Cigarette'.

The goodbye staring at us was long overdue

we were just looking for ways to say it and still

leave the door wide open for our safe return

and a possibility of a reconciliation, but there

are no goodbyes kind enough to leave lovers

or friends unscarred and unresentful. So we

are just standing here, generously giving silence

a chance to shine. I hope after we smoke this

cigarette, you would spit on the ground and

name your road, for there is no goodbye fitting

for this tragedy and its grief, and so the silence

will dance and dance until the end of our song.

Are you jealous

that I am sad

without you?

Everything we held crumbled before our eyes
and we got so caught up in fixings that we lost
sight of what was really important, like little
butterflies and little compliments that make
the sun smile, like being honest and open, and
valuing the influence of communication. Yes,
we are busy saving us, busy fixing everything,
but look at me, do you really want us to be saved?
go on, look around you, the silence, the wreck,
the ghosts, and the cold coffee you didn't touch
and didn't even say thank you to, do you really
think all this is worth saving?

Salvage yard

We were ragged and boned, and then
abandoned and loving us towards the
end was just a surrendering hour because
we were terrified of losing the haven in
us and a shoulder to lie your head on
when the day rues.

We were just scraps longing to fit in
or to belong, and we found each other
broken, and we thought putting our
halves together would make a home and
we wouldn't have to lick wounds alone.

We ignored all the sombrous messages
the universe kept sending our way, that
we were more likely unhappy together than
apart, and we chose to go against it all.

Hurricane tears

We were a thunderous storm that came
with rain and terror, and the worst thing
it took besides what we had and what we
created together, was who we were and that
we can never get back, because what it left
behind was two scarred souls wrapped in
beautiful bodies, holding onto a silhouette
of our good parts storyline that we mistook
as hope or a sign to keep fighting and we
did until we couldn't. When we look back,
we would see that we were fighting for the
same thing, just at different times and with
different tones.

Summer thieves

I miss us when we were rebels of love

and stole everything that belonged to

summer, like flowers, butterflies and

poems, and we forgot that seasons change

and that sometimes the sun doesn't care

to show up, and flowers wither, butterflies

die and nobody reads poetry anymore

and so our roads heading different paths

and we are no longer even friends, and

what we did doesn't matter now and it will

go on and on until we don't remember

each other's names.

Maybe we were too reckless
maybe we stole too much.

Grey shirt

I watched you slowly turn into a lover

I didn't fall in love with, but I knew the

good things you do when you want to

impress the person you like, and I hoped

for good days, for you to be you again

I waited for the efforts and the charming

steady gazes, and deep lustful sighs when

I would catch you looking at me, and

I waited 'til I found out that you didn't

change, that you still expressed your love

in grand ways, sadly, not towards me.

Different star signs

In the end, we were a broken mirror

and you told me to leave the shards on the floor

but I wanted to save the pieces that showed hope,

and I got a splint and incised wounds that never

really healed, because I saw us in the pieces

and we were beautifully broken

and who would want to give that all up?

and all these years I thought you ran away

because you were afraid of the cuts

and the blood, but you already knew that

there was no point in fixing something that

was meant to stay broken

and in retrospect, all the wild-wild reasons

I had, now seem rather silly and a little foreign

'cause you watched me hurt myself

and I guess that's the price I would have to pay

for not listening to your eyes and loud screams

of your silence.

"Everything works out in the end"

I held on to those words, for I was on a road

where my love story didn't have a direction

or signs leading to anything worth fighting for

and I also didn't want to quit too early or hold

on until I had nothing. I made up my mind

when it was over, that those words were all a lie

that the universe tricked me into believing

and into hoping for something that was not

even meant to be there, and only later in life

I have learned that those words were for me

and no one else and nothing else, and with

time, a part of me did *work out in the end.*

Caffeine addicts and fun stuff

We were only pieces of dawn dancing

in a poet's yard, trying to find ourselves

in each other and what we found was

not pretty, so we hid the rest

we looked at each other and we couldn't

recognise ourselves, and like fools in love,

we stayed. I think what we were truly

afraid of, was the unknown. I mean,

where to from here? I don't know

and I too am terrified.

Wounded deer

I don't want this pain to teach me a lesson

or to make me stronger. I needed someone

in the most important era of my life, to share my nights,

to borrow my body and pieces of me, and someone to

celebrate my youth with, and that *"someone"* showed up

and mostly taught me things I didn't know

I needed, like learning how to cry without

tears falling and biting the pillow instead of cursing, and

how tolerance is sometimes better than love because

love alone apparently is no longer enough, and how

messed up and yet reasonable it is to guilt

someone into staying because they owe you

your time, and *I get it* — I understand that we didn't

work out, that no promise, no fixing, no sacrifice or

compromise could've given us more time or brought

back the anxiety, the joy and the butterflies

of the day we met, but I don't need this pain

to have meaning or purpose. I want it to walk

out of my life, the same way the person who

brought it did.

I followed a satellite train once because I thought

they were stars telling me that I will be okay

I had to learn in the sickest way that nobody really stays
in your life, that no matter how many times you rip your
clothes off and offer yourself naked, even on nights when
you just to be held or sacrifice your sleep to walk them
through their dark hour, you can never keep a body that
doesn't see you as home.

And now your body is cold and worn out, and the demon
now has their eyes and their touch, and you end up mumbling
prayers that have nothing to do with you or your happiness,
but for the both of you to stay and keep trying.

You lose yourself over a flickering candlelight because
you think you are in a tunnel and very close, but you
are the moon and you don't even know, and you refuse
to open your eyes and see that you are holding onto a
ghost that feeds off your worth, and you don't even see
that you too are unhappy.

Remember the deers

I never wanted us to be over. I always believed that
I was a good person and that good things will happen
to me—*eventually,* like the day you walked into my life
when I was still grieving one of the greatest losses the
land took, and you showed up with little things that
made the day and the day after okay. I had to try everything
to stop us from ending, like turning the hourglass sideways
and forgiving you for the worst things, like making
you feel bad every time you were about to walk out
that door, and being okay with feeling small.

Different roads of eventualities, too hard to choose
which one to take that would hurt a little less, but all
of them led to me mourning the beautiful years and
only in the end, I learned that one of the good things
I was waiting for to happen, was actually you —
walking out of my life.

But who

loves

sad boys?

When you see that I can no longer handle

the hurt and I say *I love you* with red eyes

give me the last flower you have and kept

for someone else, and walk me home.

Beautiful avenue

The road is no longer weary. I guess I am

just afraid and needed an excuse to see you

and to complain more. I oftentimes find

myself missing you, and that's sad because

I would have to hate you after and relearn

to heal from you.

I gave a huge part of me to a life with you

and sometimes I would long for that part,

the laughter it has, the adventures it lived

and the memories it dearly holds.

And that part only exists with you, and

there's no way I could get it back but bear

to see it die every time we "accidentally" meet

and you would ask how am I, like you care,

do you — really care?

Wingless grieving birds

You sold me dreams

and love stories

that we only see in movies

and silly me,

I believed everything

and when the magic wore off

you had the guts to tell me

"but a road is just a road"

and you packed what's yours

and never looked back.

Settlers

I can't be here where you are going to leave me twice
yes, you are sorry now, but none of us will change and
we will wake up more resentful tomorrow, if not hurt
I happen to know how relationships end, when reasons
have run out and promises are just ghosts wishing to
die again, empty and unfulfilled. Lovers tend to flip a
coin, *heads* — we stay, *tails* — we say our goodbyes.

And when the end starts, only one is left to clean up
the dried-up rose petals that once meant something and
scrub off the melted candle on the table that its last glow
still carries old good times and your laughter, and nights
where you had to eat alone, to your very last fight.

And it says — heads
so we stay, but careful though, this one might scar us
we might hate each other *and what if we end up more
broken?* As we look for new reasons to stay and promises
we never told before, and in the meantime, we will slap
bellies and fight *again* and make up *again,* until our
next coin flip.

Sad, sad unicorns

I don't blame you anymore for being this miserable

I chose you and this life, and I recall everything smelling

like spring when I did, and I still remember your wide

smile whenever you saw me and how you never let go

of my hand.

Though most days felt like rain, the kind that always

makes one worry about a leaking roof, but then there

was always a rainbow after, *what a relief* —

and I stayed for the colours.

You chose forever being blue and never let me believe

in unicorns or pots of gold at the end, and still, I stayed for

the wide smile and good days that were only temporary,

and even you too asked me when it was over, that why

I endured it all and the answer has always been simple,

for I had no doubt and now, still, no regret.

And here it is, I loved you.

Here's to a beautiful life without you

Lovers stay lovers and friends stay friends

but only when it is meant to, and how lonely

it is, that as long as we are alive, we are yet

to figure out who is meant to stay in our lives,

and some find out in the most painful way.

Goodbyes are meant to be said or else why

would there be a whole world out there waiting

for you to explore, to celebrate and fall in love

with things you didn't know exist.

What is yours, is, and the rest is left to the wind

to take care of. I am grateful that you found me

and I found you, but we didn't stay.

Sad sky lovers

I would be reckless too and choose

to wake up in a stranger's bed, than

endure a hundred first coffee dates

and every minute of it being afraid

to be myself.

Teach me your ways of forgetting

someone you loved as soon as you

hit the road. Teach me not to hurt

and how to fall in love with someone

new and make promises after saying

goodbye to the arms that held you

no less than a month ago.

I don't want to walk anymore or sit on

a bench and wait, *show me how to fly.*

Buckwheat

I fell in love with a city that I had never been to and
somehow I know he will take care of me when I get
there. For now, we are separated by roads, towns, forests,
and life happening in between, and sometimes distance
creeps but not as deep as loneliness.

I am not running away from home, but I hope to forget
the graveyard, bodies and hearts that have hurt me and
everything I would've left behind as soon as he holds me
I hope he loves me more than the buildings, bridges and
streetlights he has known for years because I am going
to give him everything I have and it won't be enough, but
I will try to make it up to him until we both feel safe.

It's okay now, Alfie, I will leave

It's awful that we just came from attempting

to drown each other, and the only excuse we

have is that we were only trying to live, when

one of us could've just walked out that door.

Misadventures, curses and shards of make-believe

— too, trying to escape us, for we somehow managed

to make love such an ugly thing, and you are proud

because you finally made someone look in the mirror

and not recognise — themselves.

It's okay now, Alfie, I will leave

Darling

We survived the wreck too many times
that we no longer mourn butterflies that
would die on our palms and our sweet
game of using silence and cold shoulders
as a weapon, when we both only yearn
for affection.

We are afraid to hurt each other first
but we want it to sting when it does
and most times I wish we could just look
in each other's eyes and not hurt at all.

We survived the wreck more than we
deserved to, and still, we didn't learn
a thing.

Bring flowers next time

Our pictures are turning black and white

it seems, finally, the memory of you is fading

and I am glad I stopped looking for you in

sunsets, and I no longer cry whenever I hear

about your happiness. You were right, we

didn't need to shake hands, just pretending

that we never existed works too, and I am sorry

that it took me a lifetime to let you go.

Find Me In The Land

Of Venus And Milk

Maybe this is the tragic fate that befalls young lovers,

where we think we know each other so well that we see

growing up as betrayal or as growing apart. I am not

that kid anymore and so are you. It's just that change

scares you, I understand, it terrifies me too, and there

is no rush, you can take your time until you are ready,

just don't make me feel bad or stop me from trying to

figure out who I am outside your world, and when I

do, I hope you find me there.

I hope this one doesn't die on me

In my arms at 04:00 am

when coffee tastes better than wine

and memories and tears ricochet

when we have no one to toast to

but ourselves in a crowded room

and yet we feel so alone, and our

shadows on the wall would cry for us

for only now they've found out

that being alive is the hardest thing to do

it sucks to be the sad one at the

end of the day, doesn't it?

Cigarettes

We chased a dream and at some point

I woke up alone. *It turns out,* I was just

a traveller and you were a searcher.

I wish I had never missed home. I wish

I had run away with you and stayed, as

troubled as you are, but you taught me

to live with no regrets.

And today, I toast to you, to your courage,

your love that I dearly miss, and to your life

of endless possibilities and adventures.

Palm lines

Two-line poems and overeating myself
to death, whenever I remember your three
famous words, *"I love you."*
and the way you said them, the tone of your
voice and your gaze, you made them mine
and still with a broken heart, I long to hear
them and to believe them, again.

Two-line poems with your name and hating
myself for being a fool, whenever I remember
your three famous words, *"I am sorry."*
and the way you said them, shivering hands
and tears in your eyes, you made them mine
like you would die without my forgiveness
or turn into dust if I didn't let you in, again.

I didn't exist

If I get another chance in life

I will spend it looking for fame

and fortune. I will not waste it

searching for friends or for love

I will not look for you.

Coffee mug

How strange it is that our bed is still cold
and we are lying on it? *I guess* our warmth
rubbed off when we had nothing, but a
memory of past good and mean words to
say to each other, and I had to blame me all
the time to keep you. Huddles and huddles,
and no one but ourselves to cuddle, and
saying goodbye without moving *our lips.*

Where to go when loves dies

When it dies, you live reckless and
pitiful, you dance and make new
acquaintances, go to places that you
have never been, and take a sip from
a bottle of self-redemption, and for
once, everything is about you.

Kiss a stranger you just met at a bar
and kiss them all until you are ready
to love again, until you find love or
it finds you. When love dies, hopefully,
it's not yours, don't forget to leave,
don't forget to live.

The beautiful

I have arrived, and now I know what I deserve

the world and its phenomenon, *roses,* no, not roses

I want something that does not die, *the ocean,*

I deserve the ocean and all the rivers that lead

to it, and *you.*

Skulls of love

You used to hurt me while sitting on your throne

made of skulls of all your past lovers. You broke

my heart and I died, and you woke me up with your

scent because you can, with our bones wrapped

around each other and kissed by the last sunset because

you think you own me, and goodbyes you never

wanted to say. So stop apologising to my shadow while

you are still holding my corpse against my will. I only

said I loved you once and now I may never love again.

Venus

What do you do if you have found the one

and they love you the way you are supposed

to be loved and beyond, and then they die,

young, unexpectedly, like one day they are there

and an hour later, they are gone.

What do you do then? What do you do with

the love, the memories, the youth, and *the absence?*

are we not too young to die? Are we not too

young to hurt this way?

Our withering bodies

Remember me, when you share and feed

your world with shards of my heart that

led all the roads to your doorstep and footprints

of my love that guided your soul home

— *blindfolded.*

Take back the kisses and the waiting

and the burning stars and the dead butterflies

but my body and my innocence stays

for I was fire and you were rain, the sad part

of the poem where you pour and I die.

Infinite Hurrahs To Us

Broken Things

Besides you and your world, I've known nothing else,

but your grandest parties and fine liquor taught me all

I needed to know about tomorrow, people, sin, loss, grief,

and loneliness. Hurrah to you, you beautiful human.

Our end

Outside my yard, I am a garden that is married

to summer, with a smile that makes the sun lonely

and a laugh that blossoms other laughs, but in

my room, I am a withering flower and a dying moth

I am an empty grave and a corpse that still feels

and the only one who attends my funeral.

Last call

When people break up, they get drunk

and cry to happy songs, and tell their friends

what a horrible lover you were, but I don't

have friends, for your love was all I had

so I look for you in the crowd and in the music

and whenever I face the truth that I may

never get to hold you again, I either take

a stranger or a bottle home.

Owl train

Months from here, and if not, I bet a year,

our roads would cross once more and this time

you would apologise, but in a letter because you

are a coward, you have always been, and you

would tell me about your troubled life, though I

didn't even ask, you would bad mouth yourself,

you would pity yourself and blame yourself,

but all I would hear is that you only thought

of me because everyone abandoned you, because

you have no one to lean on, no one to listen to

you, no one to tolerate you, and no one

to forgive you.

Demons

We are not trying to find love

just meaningless conversations

ageing comes with demons

and thirteen rounds of drinks

a warm body for tonight

and weekend lovers, and dancing

alone to a song you just heard,

and right now it's sad to be you.

Moonwake

I am searching for a shadow that would

stay with me, even when the night arrives

and keep me safe, keep me warm, and keep

me loved, only and especially when the night

visits and when the night stays.

Pink

My happiness is temporary and so quick

that now I just sit around or go to bed

instead of enjoying the moment set for me

I am not even that obsessed with love

and relationships, they are just excuses

to keep my focus away from the demons

and the wind that never blows anything

beautiful my way.

End of our road

You took this road and I went the other way
what we were searching for, we never called
it by name. All I know is that we never saw
each other again. Seasons came and passed,
and the rain washed away who we were. Why
does falling in love when we are older so sad?

Sunsets and beer

It's funny how we prepare ourselves

for so much without knowing what

tomorrow holds. Will we even be there?

what if this is our last sunset? Okay,

you've seen and felt enough already,

but did you live? It's sad that one of

us is going to die this year.

History is all we have

I remember us as friends, I remember us as lovers

and now as strangers, sometimes I miss the roads

and the years we had, I even forget the bad ones

but this is all I have of you, *history.*

It's sad when childhood ends

It is with the greatest honour that I had

a chance to be friends with all of you, at

once and in different years. I pray that we

outlive this life thing or at least reach forty,

and I hope I die before you all, for I no

longer write funeral poems for friends and

you were the only friends this world has

blessed me with, at once and in different years

you are still and always in my heart.

It's sad when childhood ends

We Are Not Allowed

To Die Here.

I will give you the last hoot, old pal of mine

go on and drive off to the sunset, you don't

really need me for this one. Remember, we

are leaving here the same way we came and

the years are not making this departure any

easier, and not even a thousand goodbyes will

suffice. Go on, the sun is setting.

Our sorry eyes

You didn't leave the world, the world left you

for we are still here dancing around your scent

your existence still echoes and your smile remains

it's sad that we will never get to see you get old

you will be as young as your last photograph

and fulfilling as the last memory we shared with you

rivers didn't dry, trees didn't stop growing

life didn't stop living and so are roads leading

and people meeting, and people falling in love

only you disappeared and everything went on

but our world.

Hues of sunrise

For once the siren in your head dies down

and flaws have no place to shine, you try again

and be whoever you want to be, feathers of

a rare bird or wings of a foreign butterfly

a smile of a winter sun or happy petals of a

sunflower. You try again to love love and your

existence in the presence of its rise and its rays,

to its blink, its bathe and its burn, and once

more, you're alive, you befriend hope,

you are here.

Quicksand

Under your prayers,

my body succumbed to the wound

I drowned peacefully with no history

of my pain, memories too kind

to help me forget.

A candle, a party, and a road

all I know is that you fell in love

with a corpse that fell in love

with sleep.

Your ghost

In a cold room, I found you, where the sun

last smiled, still you, lonely highways, foggy streets

and a flickering lamp post, where love isn't

love anymore, but a poem you didn't even

know you wrote, figures of a man with a story

pale ageing graffiti and peeling wall paints,

lies your ghost, still haunting, still resentful

if only I could bury it too, if only my heart

could bury you too.

Jupiter's laugh

Yes, I am a drunk, I am pain,
a freak accident and a wall painted
with your blood. Isn't it strange
that I am cutting myself and you
are bleeding, that you let go of
my hand in a lake of our lifetime
tears and you are the one drowning?
you are laughing at me like a fool
like you are not the one dying.

Normal people

Do not go looking for scars
look in their eyes and listen to
their sighs, notice the lines on
their foreheads from frowning
and read the wrinkles on their
smiles. Some are good at hiding
some even believe their own lies
normal people don't exist
we are all broken, we are wild
horses, no one is healing, we are
only taking a break, standing one
foot at the end of a cliff.

For the butterflies

You found me naked once and you
loved every wrinkled flesh of my body,
every scar, every bone, every scent and
the demon hiding behind me.

Thank you for the tea in the morning
and the soup that always kissed my fever
goodbye, for the thumbs-ups and the
cuddles. Thank you for the butterflies.

Magnolia years

Some of us do not age like fine wine

but a photograph of what despair really looks like

what are we, if not survivors trying to

revive aching bones that can barely

breathe, with what's left, if not memories

that decays like seasons and quicker than

the summer haze.

Magnolia years

Dearly departed

It hurts to be you

you the one that has to live

you the one with memories

and pictures, aches, regrets

and untold goodbyes

and you know too that even

if you were given a chance to

wave, you wouldn't have said

goodbye, you would've tried

to make them stay.

Thank you

Looking back, you would still take the road less taken

go through the same pain, befriend the same faces and

wake up in places that gave you the same scars, for when

hurting was your only teacher, only then you were able

to meet you, *you are grateful.*

The Melancholy District

Is Falling

I remember all my friends who fell

I remember their laughter, jokes,

songs, stories and their rare beauty

it was not their time but they were

too good for this world anyway.

Saviel

Sometimes childhood is like a friend you had
to bury when you didn't even know death
and your parents promised you that you will
see him again but in heaven, and you always
thought they meant when you are older and
allowed to be with him, and this time without
prejudice or injury, and hope became the
closest thing to him, you could have.

You waited and longed for heaven, but it
took him only a few days to mess up the fairytale
and man, the universe has this thing of
taking everything and turning it into a stranger
all these years and you yearned for a ghost that
wasn't even yours, you haunted yourself with
his memories and his light kiss and touch. You
think he taught you love, but maybe he was
just a horny kid.

Sundays are sad

You wake up one morning more confused
and you realise you just buried a friend
you always hated goodbyes and now you have
to learn how to say them too and this time,
without crying.

Someone is singing their song and now you
miss them, you reek of regrets and wish you
could get back the days you didn't show up
when they needed you most.

Frail, burdened, holding on to memories
and sad days, that your sun rises with questions
and unwanted goodbyes.

Photographs

Memories of your smile leaning on faces of names
you don't even remember, but you recall the place
and jokes said right before those pictures were taken
 you remember that you were happy, besides the
jokes and the cold beer, you were fully content.

Surrounded by people who loved you, though it's
been years since spoken to, you don't even know
if the numbers you have of them still work and
you don't know why you stopped talking and if
you had a fight, it doesn't matter anymore because
you don't even remember what it was about,
but somebody got hurt that night, right?

Blanket

I am not strong enough to shelter you

and I am still learning to take care of myself

and to love me love you, you are too precious

to belong to a mess, to a wounded body

and a resentful heart. I pray you forgive me

and you understand that these hands were

not going to keep you safe, and this world

was not your home anyway.

All broken things return home

You don't even have to be happy
just keep going and one day everything
will be fine, *and one day never came,* and
I can't do this anymore, I don't want to.

I am exhausted and I want to disappear
Hello, home, and those who wished me
well. I am back and I am truly sorry that I
disappointed you. Please take care of me.

Anthem

We all have a breaking point

I know we have to be strong

but there is this much one can take

and sometimes it's hard to sit

right there on the frontline

and watch life itself, your friends

and opportunities pass you

and all you have is loneliness

and feeling like a failure, with

no signs of hope, and you know

you can't help yourself, you also

know that no one is going to help you

no one is coming for you

no one is looking for you.

We'd remember

I have always complained about the storm

that I stopped appreciating things that wanted

nothing from me but my presence. So I learned

to be grateful for the sunset and the rainbow

that appears at night, and fireworks too, for a

peaceful sleep and joy that awaits me in the morning

I am grateful for myself for being alive and always

being strong, and kind, and for learning from the

storm that I always complain about.

Mud pies

We didn't mourn for any of them
for the ones that remained had to
scatter around and hide from each
other, to avoid hearing each other's
suicide notes in a song or a bar fight
something was coming and the terror
of it hissed miles away.

I hid so well that at thirty, I found my
failures, ghosts of my innocence and old
toys surrounding my bed, applauding me
for outrunning the demon and for surviving
the collapse of the district and the burn.

We can't be twenty forever

Cookies and tea are tasteless when the tent is standing

in your yard and funeral hymns are sung to console you,

and before I was about to promise you that we would

understand *God's* plan one day, I was delivering a speech

at your funeral and still couldn't believe you were gone.

We can't be twenty forever

Infinite beings

As long as we are remembered, we do not die

we are born already with a story and given a timeline

we are taught songs of doom and told not to

fear the quietus of the sunset, but even if we

exit, we do not expire, for the people we met

and loved will write songs about us and write

our names on tombstones, they will celebrate

our birthdays in our absence and tell their children

to remember us when they can no longer.

Someone Has To Love

Your Ghost

To the world, I have seen everything

I needed to see. Thank you so much.

Disappear

I want to drive, just drive on an endless road

in a stormy weather but no rain. I want the cold breeze

to touch my skin, at night, so I can see the city lights

and just drive and drive, and disappear on the journey

it's about a place with no name, but where I belong

a place I could later call my home, where I would listen

to songs that would make me want to dance and cry

at the same time, different unknown faces but love

they don't know me but they are happy that *I am there.*

We'll have to love your ghost

When you are gone, we would have to

carry your body, we would have to cry

for you and we have no funeral hymns

yet prepared, we would arrive where it

is normal to write goodbyes to your bones

and to your ghost, to memories you created

and left with us, and kiss your name to

the wind.

We'll have to love your ghost

Grey

In pain, I would still smile and tell you not to worry

though you would see the difference, *but at least I am trying*

in the comfort of my bed, I would love to reminisce

on my grey-pictured memories, going to where my

smiles had disappeared, where I left my innocence

and my peace. I think I would find myself there too.

Beowulf

When you fall down, they waltz slowly
and neatly to a sombre narrated piece and
the words to the song are about you never
finding the lake of serenity and sipping
from a cup of your own tears when you
are thirsty. They stop when you seem to
get back on your feet and they stare again
and scream until your ears bleed and you
would want to break your bones. You can't
fight them, for you don't believe all this is
real or a dream, you fought your shadows
before and you ended up hurting yourself.

The South

If the God in us is asleep, He needs to wake up

for they have arrived, the South and its darkness

creeping on those who stay awake when the world

is resting, and God knows this is not our fight

the demons gather again and rejoice, for they won

they always do, and the ones disappeared with

the night are never found.

We are only here briefly

One minute you are talking and laughing

and the next minute you hear that person

has passed. The next day it's their funeral,

limited people, the service is very short like

they didn't have a life, like they didn't travel

or fall in love and break hearts. The following

day, life goes on like they never existed,

everything is so quick.

Our echoes

I hope when we meet we will hold hands

and jump around, for I reckon we will be safe

no more war, no more being defined by worldly things

and failed dreams, no more feeling alone

and if I have ever hurt you along the way, I apologise,

and I hope in the end we are all friends.

Church

Dear darkness, I am afraid but we have to call it quits

this is where you and I bid farewell, for I see the light

and I want to reclaim my shine. A list of names that

doesn't belong to human beings and church bells calling

us by name. Mama, the one you just heard was mine.

I want to die

I am falling alone in my favourite dream

the freedom of running away from my own skin

and calling reality stupid, makes me feel safe

hug me and tell me not to hold on or to be strong

that sometimes it's okay to let go.

Pluto

If I am mentioned in a memory

or pointed out in a photograph

would you say—

but I am not a person anymore

that I was too small?

if someone recalls my name

an old friend sitting on your couch

in the middle of a conversation with you,

would you say—

but I am no longer there?

sad boy politics

Everything they told you about unicorns

and pots of gold at the end of a rainbow

is still true. I know we grew up and we think

we know better, and that's what made us

so sad, but we can still believe. *Just believe.*

Dead unicorns

Old writers and philosophers tried to hide us behind beautiful words, they gave us unicorns and rainbows, summer flowers and butterflies and longing for a prince who only wants to rescue a woman and we are just a friend, but something more when he is lonely. Dead poets gave us false fairytales only so we could not see that we were dying.

Flower boy

He was a beautiful boy drowning in loneliness,

no one knew his cries, for every love story he told,

he lost a friend and another ticket closer to home

so he hanged all his tears in his backyard, but he

fell in love with a boy back in the city who kissed

his story and celebrated his scars, who planted him

flowers and kept him warm, and for a little while

he was a pig in mud, he was fireworks in the night

sky, more alive and worthy, but he had to let him go,

so he could knock on his mother's door

Kiss the sun only once

The sun kissed me back when I knew
how to be alone and now I pass my shame,
my disappointments and farewells to the
world that raised me. I spit on the face that
veneered being broken as strength instead
of teaching me love. I no longer want to be
resentful. I don't want to live in fear. I dug
my grave before, but now I set myself free.

To the world unkind

Show me an army of colours free at last

and worth celebrating, blank pages that

were supposed to be filled with suicide

notes floating in the air like a pride day

that ends with no yellow tape and blue-red

lights flashing and a crowd that is no longer

in shock, for this happens every day, if

not our spirit, they take our lives

and I will show you a corpse robbed of

its colours and a family that is not allowed

to mourn their child, because they are told

they should've seen it coming, they are told

they should've seen death coming

 I will show you the corpse of somebody's child

whose obituary was written on the day

they were born, by a country that legalised

their being and still punishes them for it.

Fairies

they are afraid of us, for we are the asylum

we are the walls and bars they built to hide us

but we find each other anyway and they get

so angry that not even dirt could bury us

beautiful criminals and grey fairies, we hand

war to love like a Monday newspaper and a cup

of tea before a kiss, and we die for it.

Life kisses goodbye

I see blood and a pile of bodies. I see children without parents and homelessness lurking, poverty and a burning land, plague and other diseases, kisses of life kissed goodbye and we are left unloved and injured. I see death walking with his long scythe trying to revive the lifeless, for he can't take so many of them, of us, he is also scared.

Everything that has cucumber is a salad

Mama prepared the table, one that looks like

our last meal. Hold hands, bow heads, and pray,

one of us is an addict, one of us is queer, one of

us is a prostitute, and one of us is a murderer,

two, Mama says it's not their fault, one, Mama

calls a free-spirited sexual goddess, *and the other one died*

which one do you think Mama never forgave?

.

Cigarette kisses

Tall, dark, beardy, beautiful eyes,

pink lips and dirty overalls, are you

going to tell my father that I kissed

a boy? But he is already disappointed

in me, so what else can he do?

disown me? but I already own my life,

and if he doesn't love me for who I am,

why should it be my loss?

Unicorns

They dance around naked and then blame us
for the bruises. They blame us for the plague
and the colours we were born with, but we died
because they said we were not real, they said we
do not exist, *bad unicorn, sad unicorn,* that man
is coming for you, quick, run away, quick, bury
yourself, you were not meant for this world *anyway.*

.

A boy who died for flowers

He was a prisoner of lost love, daffodils and a corpse
of a lonely priest, the altar called him home when he
was still a child and only wanted to make his parents
proud, but nothing he does could ever suffice.

They told him to never love a boy and he never loved again
he covered himself with bodies to survive winter and never
called again, too smart to dodge attachments and diseases
but his pillow always wept with him when the moon sang
a solace song.

ukiyo

And we run 'til we die.

The damage is done, all we have to do now

is save ourselves first and worry about people

who felt abandoned by our choice later.

Contemporary lovers

We travel dreams and mares

and fall in love with another lover

we lull our monsters to sleep

and then toast to their horror

darlings walking backwards to love

rewriting romantics and failed poets

we call old lovers at midnight

and pretend to be weak and needy

good grief, loneliness is lustful.

Visitor

You came and stayed for a little while

and I know I was not supposed to fall for you

but that's what hurting human beings do

we collapse in desire and sometimes despair

we just feel loved by the presence or efforts

we waltz around with your silhouettes and

gazes when you are not looking. You made

it clear that you were not here to stay, but

hope threw me a coin to flip and I couldn't

miss the chance, but when you waved me

goodbye with a smile, I knew I was wrong.

Sad astronauts

You used to hold me and sing me songs

that you wrote when you were seventeen

you were a sad astronaut with an abandoned ship

but space kept you safe when home couldn't

I wish I had met you then and walked with you

on your moon made of strawberries and cigarette butts

'cause nobody knows anymore how it feels

to belong to someone who keeps you safe

where did we go? *No one knows.* Why did

we leave us behind to pursue things that were

not even worth our sacrificial? *I don't know.* Sing me

your songs again and we will be seventeen.

Whiskey face

I thought of ways to hurt you back

but nothing I would do could ever

be enough. So when you are drunk

and on your way to your lonely house

made of grief and tiny pieces of your

damaged heart. I hope you fall into a

lake filled with your tears and trauma

that you handed to me to nurse, while

you were sleeping with your former

lover and still made me take care of you

and I hope you remember me before

you choke, drown and die.

Time travellers

We always give in to the universe's dare

trying to hold on to a love story that died

with us ageing and growing apart

victims of unfathomable reasons

recreating memories for a hundredth time

though we both know that we do not stay

but still, whenever we cross paths, we kiss,

and wake up in each other's arms

until we do each other's laundry, eat supper

together, and reintroduce our monsters

only to run away from each other again

because we want something true,

just not in us.

The empty room

When love is over, we remember

forlorn dreams and who we once were

sacrifices and promises gossip about us

and laugh at us for being too comfortable

and everything we left behind to be here

now has a road and a story, a quest and a purpose

anything but to stay and try again.

Moon lovers

We used to think that it was poetic

when we watched the moon together

but cities, bodies and hearts apart

oh, we were just sad and lonely beings

we were cowards and afraid to love

and get hurt again, that we thought

isolating ourselves kept us safe

but when were we going to live?

we told ourselves that it was fate

that we found each other until we believed it

but we were only excuses and delays

we kept each other close and gave our love

to the moon to make dying alone not so tragic,

but we didn't have to be alone.

Dirty palms

It's just something we say when the fire

comes blazing on everything we've built

it was never our fault but regrets sang a

chorus that held our bedroom fights

I hoped someday we would laugh about it

roasting marshmallows and memories

the sad face of summer rain and nostalgia

burning old photographs with our grievance

and worshipping cradle songs

violent caresses and desperate whispers

everything the flame touched yearned

for the promises we made when we were still

afraid to lose each other

and our bad choices applauded our resilience

for we keep saying, *"I've been waiting for you"*

but we ran away when we should've rebuilt.

Paper Romance

We were still fragile when we met

so we let cities, roads and time

balance our flammable attachments

we administered each other's damages

and used love letters to fill up the void

it was us against 21st-century romance

but sometimes bodies need to be held

and heavy-sighed calls and drunk texts,

promises to meet one day and kiss for hours

can never win against lovers who run

together in the night rain, holding hands

we learned to appreciate distance apart

but we were not meant to die alone.

Marry me with Saturn's ring

I think we worshipped the fire far too long

that we only see beauty in things that burn,

break and fall, in grief and wingless blackbirds

I don't care what the universe writes about me

I didn't belong to it anyway, for I danced with

monsters and I fell in love, got hurt and went back

again with bruises and came out more broken

but I held on to dear life when it came to warm

bodies and folklores of loneliness, and I sure will

do it again. The toasts, the friends, the sun, take

us to a place where we are born with nothing

but a name, and let erasure take care of us again

for you said you loved me and I ran away.

We Were Never Ugly,

to begin with

I wish we had known in the old world

that we were more beautiful because we loved

unafraid even when we were broken.

A field full of wildflowers

It's not safe where you are, throwing butterflies
my way. I need you to know I too am broken, I can
burn your pity world in a blink. The fairytale is
fading away 'cause reality is staring us in the eye,
you are now twenty-nine, this close to your end
and I can't even cry 'cause I am busy loving you
with bated breath and ticking time. How I wish
we were still lying in a field full of wildflowers.

The boy I left behind

If only he knew this colourful world is still grey

that he will have to grow up and be miserable

that loneliness and being alone are completely

different places that darkness proudly owns

and he will make sad clichès run for their money

friends will be hard to find and so are darlings

for some just take and take, some leave and some die

and birthdays are love letters from death to remind you

that you are only getting closer to him.

Honeymoon bears

We chased butterflies all our lives, that they landed us
in these arms, we kissed borrowed lovers so many times
that we learned how important it is to be present and
how comfortable it is to sleep on separate pillows, for
the only time we are not responsible for each other's
happiness is when our eyes are closed, but can still feel
each other's heartbeats, that a little space doesn't mean
we are angry and vulnerability is like a meal made by
Grandma, made with frozen rain and dancing rainbows
our history is a teacher that never grows old or dies,
and it constantly teaches us that if we are ready, we can
always find our way to each other. Only if we are ready.

The orbiter

I always found you close, circling your way

around my existence, and most nights I felt

like a beeping star, especially when the darkness

claimed its right. I could hear your heart beating

for me a mile away, with your told history of

a taker and a coward, but you made it sound

so romantic, like someone afraid of love

because you once gave everything you had to

someone who was not ready, and all I wanted

to do was wrap you around my comfort and

my warmth, and feed you all the butterflies in

my spring and my garden, only to find out in

the end that you were orbiting different stars all

at once to see which one was desperate, easy and

willing to let you take, and you took from me

and I was still too in love to realise that I searched

and asked for you even after you abandoned me

and left me with nothing, only to learn in the

saddest way that you never loved me, 'cause when

I found you, you only gave me a flatline

The quiet that romance leaves

You coward in the presence of terror like you were never taught to clip butterfly wings to make yourself not cry when love crawls away from you. You were raised like a wounded soldier but you crumble whenever death visits you give him everything you built and beg him for more time, you throw roses at his feet and kiss his footprints things you should do when love comes by, but you choose to cuddle with regrets instead and sing blues to goodbyes because you are afraid of the arguments that own your nights and bedroom romance right before the storm takes you are afraid of the pain, quietness and loneliness that the storm leaves behind.

Time is a mean friend

I have been where the wild things are

I atoned for all the horrors I brought to

this land and to you, and when I was

hungry, I licked my burning wounds

you said I must wait, that I will heal

only when you are ready. I have waited,

though all I got so far were little hours

in a week, where I would forget the

pain, but I would remember it again

when it's quiet. This is not healing, do

something, and now you are saying that

I should forgive myself, but how the hell

do I do that with all these scars?

our last cigarette

When I wrote to your ghost

I was sleeping with the first stage of grief

and he looked at me with your gaze and

your promise. He made the reality of loss

feels like something one can wake up

from, and besides dreaming of you every

moon, I could only draw your face with

my yearningness and I wrote to how I

remembered you, for I already knew you

were still alive way before old friends said

they saw you in a place where love is a

drunk stranger who wishes luck to hearts

that beat names, faces and reminiscences

I knew you were above ground and still

taking a piss at life, for when I danced

with melancholia for the first time, he said,

it felt like we'd met before, and we did,

because he danced with you before me.

Widowed birds

We danced with each other's ghosts on

a broken glass to a slow ballad sung by

our past and undiscovered planets. We

were strangers before, because we knew

how to fly and we were strangers after,

for we thought we knew we could find

our way home, but in our absence, we

longed and grieved each other, we kissed

our dreams, hoping we would find ourselves

in each other's cuddle, but the more we

searched our way back and the more

we befriended the sky, we stopped loving

and living, we became temporary creatures

and withered everything we touched, we

became sad and unreliable. *What a waste,*

for we died worlds apart anyway.

The altar of an abandoned chapel

We gave fairytale a party and another reason to dance
and it's okay when soulmates don't wake up next to
each other. What's important is that they had a chance
to fall in love, a chance to hold hands, kiss, and share a
favourite song, a chance to wipe each other's tears and
a chance to say goodbye. Little, big things that the
universe deny yearning hearts.

The morgue

My body is warm, but still shivers to the cold

cold-hearted world cuts and we will never be the

same, dynamites that never explode, but ready

we are the masterpiece of terror with no asylum

banging nails on wood, creating our own coffins

ready — to die with no signs of heaven or hell

or somewhere else to be, but here, dark clouds

hovering, our skin, illuminating, warm, the

darkness and cold, haunting us, do not tell me,

our souls will still be wandering this land, my

soul, still suffering.

Hopefully, with many coming books, 'Our Last Cigarette' will be accompanied by the following collective titles;

1. Our Last Kiss.

2. Our Last Beer.

3. Our Last Butterflies.

4. Our Last Words.

5. Our Last Sunset.

6. Our Last Sleep.

7. Our Last Everything.

8. *And many more.*

1. Salvaged yard.

2. Hurricane tears.

3. Summer thieves.

4. Grey shirt.

5. Different star signs.

6. "Everything works out in the end."

7. Caffeine addicts and fun stuff.

8. Wounded deers.

9. I followed a satellite train once because I thought they were stars telling me that I will be okay.

10. Remember the deers.

11. Beautiful avenue.

12. Wingless grieving birds.

13. Settlers.

14. Sad, sad unicorns.

15. Here's to a beautiful life without you.

16. Sad sky lovers.

17. It's okay, Alfie, I will leave.

18. Buckwheat.

19. Darling.

20. Bring flowers next time.

21. I hope this one doesn't die on me.

22. Cigarettes.

23. Palm lines.

24. I didn't exist.

25. Coffee mug.

26. Where to go when love dies.

27. The beautiful.

28. Skulls of love.

29. Venus.

30. Our withering bodies.

31. Our end.

32. Last call.

33. Owl train.

34. Demons

35. Moonwake.

36. Pink.

37. End of our road.

38. Sunsets and beer.

39. History is all we have.

40. It's sad when childhood ends.

41. Our sorry eyes.

42. Hues of sunrise.

43. Quicksand.

44. Your ghost.

45. Jupiter's laugh.

46. Normal people.

47. For the butterflies.

48. Magnolia years.

49. Dearly departed.

50. Thank you.

51. Saviel.

52. Sundays are sad.

53. Photographs.

54. Blankets.

55. All broken things return home.

56. Anthem.

57. Mud pies.

58. We can't be twenty forever.

59. We'd remember

60. Infinite beings.

61. Disappear

62. We'll have to love your ghost.

63. Grey.

64. Beowulf.

65. The South.

66. We are only here briefly.

67. Our echoes.

68. Church.

69. I want to die.

70. Pluto.

71. Dead unicorns.

72. Flower boy.

73. Kiss the sun only once.

74. To the world unkind.

75. Life kisses goodbye.

76. Everything that has cucumber is a salad.

77. Cigarette kisses.

78. Fairies.

79. Unicorns.

80. A boy who died for flowers.

81. Contemporary lovers.

82. Visitor.

83. Sad astronauts.

84. Whiskey face.

85. Time travellers.

86. The empty room.

87. Dirty palms.

88. Moon lovers.

89. Paper romance.

90. Marry me with Saturn's ring.

91. A field full of wildflowers.

92. The boy I left behind.

93. Honeymoon bears.

94. The orbiter.

95. The quiet that romance leaves.

96. Time is a mean friend.

97. When I wrote to your ghost.

98. Widowed birds.

99. The altar of an abandoned chapel.

100. The morgue.